Princess Penelope and the Runaway Kitten

nosy crow

Happy Christmas
2018
to
Martha

love from
Zanna
&
Grandad x

Alison Murray

In Royaltown Palace one long lazy day,
Princess Penelope wanted to play.
But Daddy was reading
and Mummy was knitting,
so she thought she'd make friends
with the mischievous kitten.
Penelope giggled – the kitten looked funny
with pink wool all tangled
around his white tummy!

But then off he ran, with a swish of his tail,
leaving behind him a pink woolly trail.
Penelope chased him, and Doggy came too . . .

. . . the cage door swung open and out the birds flew!

They looked in the throne room
and round the gold chairs.

But where was the kitten?

He'd dashed to the stairs!

Penelope followed
the trail up and down.

"Where can he have got to?"
she said, with a frown.

She rushed to the garden.
"I think that it's clear
our runaway kitten has
had fun around here!"

And then the tired princess sat down with a bump . . .

. . . while the kitten escaped with a skip and a jump.

Penelope followed. "Oh, please come back, Kitty!

The wool will be ruined, and it was so pretty!"

But the kitten went scampering
past the tall trees,
and on through the cabbages,
spinach and peas.

The parlour maid squealed and dropped the cakes on the floor.

Then Penelope spotted him dash through a door.

"There you are!"
said the princess.
"Let's sort out
this muddle!"

. . . but the kitten was having a sleep and a cuddle.

For Lesley
A.M.

First published in 2013 by Nosy Crow Ltd

The Crow's Nest, 10a Lant Street

London SE1 1QR

www.nosycrow.com

This edition published 2015

ISBN 978 0 85763 655 3

A CIP catalogue record for this book is available

from the British Library.

Printed in China by Imago

Papers used by Nosy Crow are made from

wood grown in sustainable forests.

1 3 5 7 9 8 6 4 2